Halfway Up the Mountain

by Theo E. Gilchrist
Pictures by Glen Rounds

A Lippincott I-Like-To-Read Book

J.B. Lippincott Company
Philadelphia and New York

U.S. Library of Congress Cataloging in Publication Data

Gilchrist, Theo E
    Halfway up the mountain.

    (A Lippincott I-like-to-read book)
    SUMMARY: An old woman's method of cooking beef also rids her of
Bloodcoe the bandit.
    [1. Robbers and outlaws—Fiction. 2. Cookery—Fiction] I. Rounds, Glen,
birth date II. Title.
PZ7.G384Hal   [E]   77-29020
ISBN-0-397-31805-7

FOR JEREMY AND ALICE

Over the green hill and across the blue river, in a shack halfway up the mountain, there lived an old man and an old woman.

Though the old man was slow of movement, the old woman didn't mind. Though the old woman was almost blind, the old man didn't mind. Hand in hand they greeted the sunrise. Hand in hand they greeted the sunset.

They were happy except for one
thing. Day after day the old woman
cooked the very same meal. It was
   Salt the beef, pepper the beef,
   Push the garlic bits inside,
   Boil and flavor with vinegar water.

Now this the old man did mind.
"Woman," he said, "fried chicken
would taste good. Roast pork, even
better. Why can't you change?"

The old woman replied softly, "I know the salt shaker by the nick in its side. I know the pepper by its rough wood holder. The garlic I find by its powerful perfume, the vinegar by its tang. And you cut a slab of beef for me each morning. How could I change?"

Now, this sameness of taste was
making the old man tetchy. He
decided to go down the mountain a
piece and ask advice of the spirit who
lived in the oldest aspen tree.

Slowly the old man approached the tree. "O Great One, listen."

The tree quaked. In a silver whisper it said, "Speak, old man."

"My old woman is a good woman,
but day after day she makes the same
food. It's
    Salt the beef, pepper the beef,
    Push the garlic bits inside,
    Boil and flavor with vinegar water.
How can I get her to change?"

The tree's leaves trembled. With a whish of a sigh, it said, "There are worse things than beef."

13

The tree said no more.

The old man was disappointed. He
dragged himself back home.

That night the old man lay on the
pallet on the floor beside the old
woman. In her sweet sleep she saw
red bearberries and blue larkspur.

15

He dreamed of baked ham. When
he tried to eat some, the ham
changed into a monstrous pig. It
rushed at him with a snort and a
snuffle until he begged to wake.

As he lay there, the old man heard
sounds far away—twigs snapping,
little stones chipping loose and
rolling down the mountain.

Then the noise became louder. A
cannon of a voice boomed into song.
    "With a jingle of gold,
       a gurgle of rum—
    Fall to your knees,
       Bloodcoe has come!
    I'm beastly, I'm bloody, I'm bad."

The old man trembled with fear. He had heard tales of Bloodcoe the bandit. Bloodcoe had burned barns and broken bones. It was said he was more monster than man.

"Oh, crimey!" Now the voice was
very near. "Where's me bottle?
Come, good rum, give strength to me
walking and sound to me singing.
   I'm the terror of the countryside,
   Gold's me business, booze me bride.
   I'm beastly,
      I'm bloody,
         I'm ba-a-ad!"

With a crash, the door swung open.
The huge outline of the bandit
swayed in the doorway.

21

"Ho, now, what's this?" Bloodcoe
poked the bottle into the old man's
side.

"It's just me, an old man, and my
old wife," the old man cried. "Don't
hurt us."

Bloodcoe yawned. "We'll see about
that. Now, out with you. There's no
room for three in here."

The old man helped the old
woman up. He led her to the cattle
shed.

"We'll sleep on the straw here,
good old woman," he said. She didn't
seem to waken at all.

25

The old man lay there trembling.
He heard crashing and cursing.
"This blasted floor's too cold for
sleeping. Ah, the stove's the place.
The coals inside are still warm. Bully
for you, Bloodcoe."

Soon snores came thundering
from the shack. The old man finally
fell asleep.

A little before dawn, the old
woman wakened. She felt the straw
and heard the noises of the cattle.
She realized she was in the shed.

"Old man," she whispered, "why
are we here?" But the old man slept
on.

The old woman sighed and sat awhile. "I'll let him be," she reasoned, "and do as usual."

Slowly she arose and made her way to the shack. It didn't matter that she could hardly see. Her feet knew the stony path well.

The old woman pushed open the door and found her way to the stove. She had left the old man asleep. But he must have been up very early, for a mound of beef lay there on the stove.

She rolled up her sleeves. She felt the nick in the side of the salt shaker and shook it hard. She fingered the rough wood pepper holder and showered pepper all around. Then she started to push garlic bits inside the beef.

All at once came a great scream
and such sneezing as she had never
heard. "Waaaaaaah!" boomed the
voice. Bloodcoe leaped down off the
stove and tore out the door. "Me eyes
are burning out of me head. Me ribs
are broken. And the smell! The
smell! The devil himself is in that
place!"

34

He bawled and shouted and ran
and stumbled until the wind brought
back only a faint, distant wail.

The old man was startled by the noise. He sat bolt upright and blinked. He reached for his wife's hand but found her gone.

As best he could, he hurried to the shack. "What happened, old woman?"

"Old man, the beef for today's
dinner wasn't dead yet. I did as
usual—

Salt the beef, pepper the beef,
Push the garlic bits inside.

But before I could put the vinegar
water on to boil, the beef got itself up
off the stove. It ran out the door with
the noise of a whole herd."

On the stove lay an empty rum
bottle and two bags. The old man
shook one of the bags. There was a
cheerful clink.

41

"Well done, old woman!" he said.
"That wasn't beef you treated with
pepper and garlic. That was the
bandit Bloodcoe himself. He forced
us out of our home last night, but he
paid well for his lodging. He left two
bags of gold."

"Well then, old man, you can go down the mountain. Buy yourself some chicken or pork if that's what you fancy."

"Some other day, maybe," he said.
"But for now, old woman, one thing I
know."

"What is that?"

He put his arms around her.

"I know, old woman, that there are worse things than beef."

Hand in hand they greeted the sunrise, thankful for each other, thankful for the start of a new day.

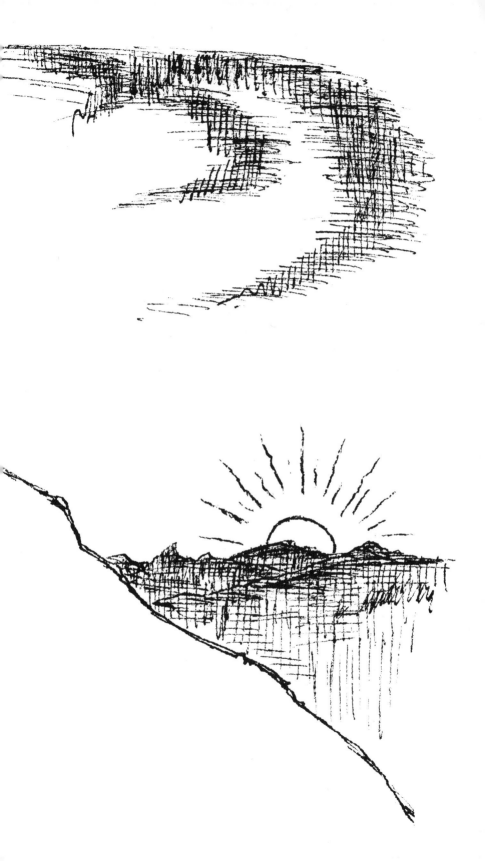

THEO E. GILCHRIST is a librarian whose specialty is working with children. Her poems and stories have appeared in numerous magazines. Ms. Gilchrist and her husband live in White Bear Lake, Minnesota. They have two children.

GLEN ROUNDS attended art school in Kansas City, Missouri, and in New York City, and now lives in Southern Pines, North Carolina. He has illustrated many books for young people.